THE PYTHON PROBLEM

PET VET
Book #1 CRANKY PAWS
Book #2 THE MARE'S TALE
Book #3 MOTORBIKE BOB
Book #4 THE PYTHON PROBLEM

First American Edition 2010
Kane Miller, A Division of EDC Publishing

First published by Scholastic Australia Pty Limited in 2009
This edition published under license from Scholastic Australia Pty Limited.
Text copyright © Sally and Darrel Odgers, 2009
Interior illustrations © Janine Dawson, 2009
Cover copyright © Scholastic Australia, 2009
Cover design by Natalie Winter

For information contact:
Kane Miller, A Division of EDC Publishing
P.O. Box 470663
Tulsa, OK 74147-0663
www.kanemiller.com
www.edcpub.com

Library of Congress Control Number: 2009931233

Printed and bound in the United States of America
1 2 3 4 5 6 7 8 9 10
ISBN: 978-1-935279-16-7

THE PYTHON PROBLEM

Darrel & Sally Odgers

Illustrated By Janine Dawson

Kane Miller
A DIVISION OF EDC PUBLISHING

Welcome to
Pet Vet Clinic!

My name is Trump, and Pet Vet
Clinic is where I live and work.

At Pet Vet, Dr. Jeanie looks after
sick or hurt animals from the town
of Cowfork as well as the animals
that live at nearby farms and stables.

I live with Dr. Jeanie in Cowfork
House, which is attached to the
clinic. Smaller animals come to Pet

1

Vet for treatment. If they are very sick, or if they need operations, they stay for a day or more in the hospital ward which is at the clinic.

In the morning, Dr. Jeanie drives out on her rounds, visiting farm animals that are too big to be brought to the clinic. We see the smaller patients in the afternoons.

It's hard work, but we love it. Dr. Jeanie says that helping animals and their people is the best job in the world.

Staff at the Pet Vet Clinic

Dr. Jeanie: The vet who lives at Cowfork House and runs Pet Vet Clinic.

Trump: Me! Dr. Jeanie's Animal Liaison Officer (A.L.O.), and a Jack Russell terrier.

Davie Raymond: The Saturday helper.

Other Important Characters

Dr. Max: Dr. Jeanie's grandfather. The retired owner of Pet Vet Clinic.

Major Higgins: The visiting cat. If he doesn't know something, he can soon find out.

Whiskey: Dr. Max's cockatoo.

Patients

Diamond: A lost diamond python.

Peter Wu: A Siamese cat.

Map of Pet Vet Clinic

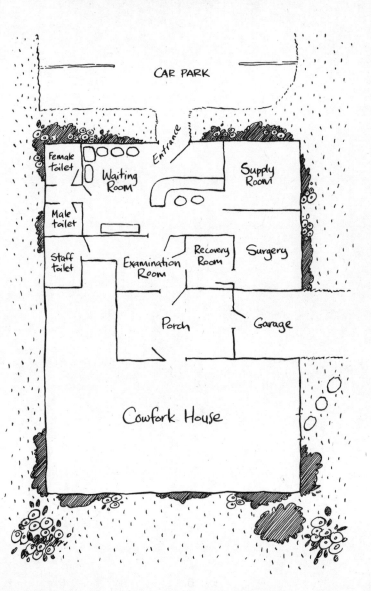

Chapter 1

"Follow That Van!"

I was out for a walk with Davie, our Saturday helper.

Mostly Dr. Jeanie takes me for walks, but today she was busy with **accounts**, so Davie took me instead.

> **Accounts** – Lists of money coming in and going out of a business.

We were about to turn into Cobber Street when we saw a battered looking van, the kind with two doors at the back, coming slowly up the road. The driver kept looking from side to side. "I wonder if he's lost?" said Davie.

The van rattled a lot, and the smell of the exhaust made me sneeze as the driver pulled up beside us. He rolled down the window and leaned out. He wasn't much older than Davie.

"Hey, mate, I'm looking for Frog Street," said the driver. "The map says it should be here, but the sign there says Cobber Street."

"It's both," said Davie. "This end is Cobber Street. The other end is Frog Street. Whose house are you looking for?"

"My friend's aunt's. She's moving in to number 59 today and I offered to bring some of her stuff. It wouldn't all fit in the mover's truck, so I packed it in my old van."

Davie nodded. "Drive on up this street and turn in at the other end. There's a bridge over a kind of gully with a creek, and trees and long grass growing down the slope. You'll see the sign."

"Thanks." The driver rolled up the window and took off. I sneezed again and shook my head to get the rattle out of my ears.

Davie fanned blue exhaust fumes away with his hand. "That old van needs some work on the engine," he said.

We were walking on when the van jerked and turned sharply

around the corner. One of the back doors swung open with a jolt. Davie and I stared as a large glass tank tumbled out and smashed on the side of the road, just before the bridge. The van kept on driving and was soon out of sight.

"Follow that van!" yelled Davie, and we broke into a run.

Of course, we stopped when we got to the tank. It looked like a fish tank, but there was no water on the road, just some bits of wood and lumps of rock. I sniffed a piece of wood. It had a strange, musty scent that made my **hackles** itch.

Davie pulled me back. "Careful, Trump. Don't tread on the broken glass." He looked around. "We'd better tell that driver what happened." He tugged on my leash. I wanted to follow the strange scent, but Davie insisted I go with him.

We ran on over the bridge and along to number 59, where the driver was just getting out of the van.

Hackles
(HACK–'lls) – We dogs can lift the hair on our necks and down our backs. We do this when we are nervous or angry, to make ourselves look bigger and more fierce.

"Hello again," he said to Davie. "Is anything wrong?"

"You dropped something out of the back of the van," said Davie.

"The door burst open when you turned."

The driver sighed. "Thought I'd fixed that. Better go back and pick it up."

"Not much point," said Davie. "It was a tank, and it's all smashed up. We'd better get the glass off the road, though. Might cause an – What's wrong?"

The driver was staring at him. "You mean the *snake* tank fell out?"

"Um …" Davie stood on one leg. "I thought it was an empty fish tank."

The driver groaned. "It was a snake tank, and it wasn't empty. It had a python in it."

"Oh," said Davie. "We didn't see any python, just the smashed tank."

The driver groaned again. "Of all the things that could have fallen out, it had to be the *snake tank*. I don't suppose you've got a bag or something to catch it in?"

"No," said Davie. "Just my **work gloves**." He pulled the gloves out of his pocket. "I work at Pet Vet Clinic," he added.

> **Work gloves –** People who work with animals often wear heavy leather gloves to protect their hands from bites and pecks.

"Well, I hope you're good at catching snakes," said the driver. He grabbed a cardboard box out of the van and we all hurried back the way we'd come.

We crossed the bridge again. The smashed tank was still there. I really wanted to investigate the strange scent, but Davie tied my leash to a railing. All I could do was sit and watch as he and the driver looked around, using sticks to poke into the long grass and shrubs growing down the bank near the little creek. I whined and barked to let Davie

know I wanted to help, but he told me to be quiet.

"You might cut yourself, Trump. Then Dr. Jeanie would have to patch you up," he said. "Trump belongs to the vet I work for," he told the driver.

They searched for a long time. I heard them talking, but I couldn't make out what they were saying. At last they came back up the bank. Davie put on his gloves and he and the driver picked up as much glass as they could find and piled it in the box.

The driver sighed. "I'd better get back to the van. Thanks for your help, Davie."

"Sorry we didn't find it," said

Davie. He put his gloves back in his pocket and untied my leash. I tried to sniff the bits of wood and rock still lying around, but Davie said we had to go.

Dr. Jeanie had finished the accounts when we got back to Pet Vet. "Good walk?" she asked us, unclipping my leash.

"We didn't go far," said Davie, and he sat down to tell her about the python.

I wanted to go right back to sniff around, but I knew if I tried Davie or Dr. Jeanie would call me back. Instead, I trotted off to Dr. Max's cottage to consult his cockatoo, Whiskey, about pythons.

Trump's Diagnosis. Pets get nervous when they have to move to a new home. Even a sensible pet might run away if it escapes from a moving van. Then it is likely to get lost, because there are no familiar scents to follow. If you move, make sure your pet is kept secure until you have time to settle it in its new home.

CHAPTER 2

Pythons, According to Whiskey

When I arrived at the cottage, Dr. Max was digging in his garden. He patted me, and rubbed my ears with an earthy hand. "Hello, Trump. How's my best terrier girl?"

I waved my tail to tell him I was well.

Whiskey was digging too. He'd made quite a burrow in the soft earth, so all I could see were his tail feathers. They jerked sideways with every shovel of his beak.

I like to dig, so I helped him.

"Wharrrrrrk!" yelled Whiskey, poking his head out of his burrow. "What *are* you doing, Dog?"

Oops. When Whiskey calls me "Dog" instead of "Trump" it's time to stand well back. Whiskey has never pecked me yet, but that's because I respect his beak.

"I was helping you dig," I said, backing away.

Whiskey waddled forward and shook out his wings, spraying me with fine soil and **feather dust**. Then he pushed his beak up close to my nose.

> **Feather dust –** Cockatoos have a special powdery dust in their feathers.

"Get this straight, Dog. Digging a burrow is serious business for a cockatoo. It has to be done just right, so keep your paws to yourself!"

"I'll remember," I said. I sat down. "Whiskey?"

Whiskey shook his wings again. He sounded like Dr. Jeanie's clothesline on a windy day. Some of the feather dust tickled my nose and I sneezed. "What is it, Trump?"

"What are you digging *for*?"
I asked. "I dig for bones, or to
exercise my paws, or because the
earth is soft, or because something
might be hiding in a hole."

"*I* dig for grubs," said Whiskey.
"Also for tasty roots. Also for – but
I'm sure you didn't come here to
discuss digging habits, Trump."

I told him about the python.
"So," I finished, "what are pythons
like, Whiskey?"

"Pythons are big snakes."

Big snakes! I wasn't so happy about
that. Like some other animals, snakes
bite if they are scared or upset. Some
of them are very dangerous.

Whiskey continued. "Back when
Dr. Max and I were young, Old

Bushy Applebloom kept a python in his hut. He used it for rodent control. I used to see it when we went to look at Bushy's dog."

"What was it like?" I asked.

"I only saw the head end, poking out of a corner." Whiskey waggled his tail feathers and picked his beak with one claw. "I didn't like the way it looked at me."

"What did you say to it?"

"Nothing," said Whiskey. "Pythons don't have any ears."

"Neither do you."

"Of course I have ears, you foolish terrier. I just don't flap them around in the breeze like a dog!" Whiskey turned his head. I peered closely and saw a small dark hole in among the feathers. "Anyway, snakes don't have ears, so they can't hear. That means they don't say much."

"You mean I could yap at a snake hole all I liked and the snake wouldn't know?"

"It would know, and don't you forget it! Snakes feel sound as a vibration. They also smell with their tongues."

I stuck my tongue out and pulled it back in. "Did this snake you used to see ever try to bite you?"

"No. I perched on Dr. Max's shoulder. Pythons do bite, but they don't poison you like other kinds of snakes."

"Where is a lost python likely to go?"

"Down a hole, or in a tree, or on a rock in the sun maybe," said Whiskey.

"*I* don't know, Trump! If you take my advice you won't look for it."

"It's lost," I argued. "I am Dr. Jeanie's A.L.O., and it's my duty to help and support other animals. And you said it wouldn't poison me."

"Some bigger pythons can *eat* small dogs," said Whiskey. "Don't risk it, Trump. I wouldn't like to see your tail vanishing down a python."

Neither would I, I thought, checking the end of my tail.

Dr. Max stuck his fork in the ground and put his hand on the middle of his back. "That's enough for today," he said. "I think it's going to rain. Come on, Whiskey." He bent and held out his hand. Whiskey stepped onto his wrist and marched up Dr. Max's sleeve to sit on his shoulder. His dark eyes swiveled down to look at me. "Don't risk it, Trump," he said again, as Dr. Max carried him into the cottage.

Trump's Diagnosis. Like dogs, cockatoos like to be higher than other animals. Most tame cockatoos will walk up your arm to sit on your shoulder. Be careful if a cockatoo climbs up your arm. Their claws are strong and sharp, and some of them peck.

Caught in the Rain

I didn't want to go back to the clinic just yet. I decided to go back and look for the python. I intended to be *very* careful.

I made my way back towards Frog Street. I made sure not to let Davie and Dr. Jeanie see me, because I knew they would call me back. Soon I was sniffing at the bits of rock and wood that had been in the tank. The musty scent was strong. I remembered I'd smelled something like it when Dr. Jeanie took me walking in the bush. Snake!

I felt my hackles rise. Most animals are a bit scared of snakes. I was a bit nervous about my paws, too. Davie and the driver had cleared up the mess, but here and there a tiny bit of glass glittered. I backed away from the glass and tried to detect the scent. The python must have slithered away as soon as the tank broke, but its scent was overlaid by Davie's and the driver's.

I peered down the slope of the gully leading to the creek. Maybe the python had gone there to hide. I followed my nose into the long grass and buttercups, and snapped at a mosquito. I was still nosing around when I heard Dr. Jeanie call.

I was busy. It would be easy to pretend I hadn't heard. But maybe Dr. Jeanie wanted me for something important. We might have a patient who needed an A.L.O. Or maybe the butcher had given Dr. Jeanie a meaty beef bone for me. Or it might be time to go to the park.

I had a final sniff around, then headed back to Pet Vet. A few drops of rain splattered on my head. More bounced on the footpath, making wet splotches. The smell of wet cement rose, so strong even a human would smell it. I broke into a gallop, but I was dripping when I got home.

"Oh, Trump, just look at you!" said Dr. Jeanie. "You're filthy!"

I looked down at myself. Dr. Jeanie

was right. My paws are usually white, but now they were dark brown with mud. I had bits of grass stuck to my sides, and brown blotches and speckles on me that didn't belong. I lifted one paw and whined, then licked my leg to show Dr. Jeanie I would clean myself.

"You're dripping," said Dr. Jeanie. "What on earth have you been doing? I thought you were with Dr. Max!" She picked me up and carried me through to the big sink. "In you go!" She dumped me in the sink, then ran warm water over my back. "Davie, bring the dog soap, please!" she called.

I don't like baths, but I had to put up with it. Struggling and kicking

would get me nowhere. Running
off scattering suds and dirty water
is not behavior that befits an A.L.O.
Besides, it would annoy Dr. Jeanie.
I sat in the sink and quivered while
Dr. Jeanie soaped me. I had a warm
rinse, then Dr. Jeanie turned off the
tap and pressed water out of my
coat with her hands. She dried me
with a rough towel, and rubbed
my nose. "That's better. Now stay

inside, Trump. I don't want you wandering off again."

I was still shaking myself when the clinic doorbell rang.

Dr. Jeanie took off her apron and walked through to unbolt the door. I followed, leaving damp paw prints on the floor.

"Are you the vet?" I didn't recognize the woman's voice, so I knew it wasn't one of our regular clients.

"Yes," said Dr. Jeanie. "I'm Jeanie Cowfork. We're closed on Saturdays, but I can see your pet if it's an emergency. Otherwise please make an appointment for next week."

"It's a kind of emergency," said the woman.

"Come in out of the rain," said

Dr. Jeanie. She stepped back so the woman could come inside. "Is the patient in your car or at home?"

"I don't know where he is," said the woman, taking off her long coat. "That's the problem. I'm Hayley Seeney, and we've just moved down here. A friend of my nephew's offered to bring some of our things in his van, but you'll never believe what happened."

Dr. Jeanie smiled. "Oh, I think I can guess. Your nephew's friend packed your pet python in its tank instead of putting it in a proper cage or bag."

"Oh." Hayley sounded surprised. "You heard about Diamond already?"

"News travels quickly around here," said Dr. Jeanie. "Especially when my Saturday helper is a witness to the accident. Davie went straight to the tank when it fell, but he said your python had already gone."

"I see." Hayley bent and clicked her fingers to me. "Hello, girl."

I went to sniff her hand, then wagged my tail. I could tell she was a nice person, and that she was worried.

"This is my friend Trump, who also witnessed the accident," said Dr. Jeanie. "Your python wasn't the only animal out and about in the rain this morning. I'm sorry to hear you haven't found it yet."

"Not a trace," said Hayley. "That's why I came to you. If Diamond gets hurt, someone might think a vet is the place to bring him."

"He's a diamond python, I suppose?"

Hayley nodded. "He's not big, as diamonds go." She held out her hands, far apart.

"That's bigger than the local snakes," said Dr. Jeanie. "I don't know much about pythons. Most of my patients are dogs and cats, the occasional guinea pig and farm animals like cattle and ponies. What's your Diamond like to handle?"

"I've had him for several years, and he's quite tame with me. I don't know how he'd react if someone strange grabbed him." Hayley sighed. "He's not a danger to anyone, except maybe a chicken or a small rabbit, but I'm afraid people might think he's out to get them, or their pets. Do you have any advice?"

"He's probably found shelter," said Dr. Jeanie. "I'll take down your details and let you know if someone brings him in or reports a sighting. I think your best move is to spread the news. If the locals *know* there's a non-poisonous snake on the loose they're less likely to panic if they see him."

"They won't be pleased if he takes up residence in a henhouse," said Hayley Seeney.

"Neither will the hens," said Dr. Jeanie.

Trump's Diagnosis. Like animals, humans are usually scared of snakes. It is a bad idea to grab any snake, even if you are sure it's not poisonous. If you see one in the wild, leave it alone. If one comes into your garden, keep away and tell someone sensible.

CHAPTER 4

SPREADING THE NEWS

"Well, well," said Dr. Jeanie when Hayley had gone. "Life is never dull at Pet Vet, is it, Trump?" She took a large sheet of paper from the desk and made a poster to pin up in the clinic. On it was a picture of a python and Hayley Seeney's name and address. "We'd better see what we can find out about pythons," she told Davie. "In case anyone has questions."

"They'll have questions," said Davie.

He was right.

It rained all the way through Sunday. On Monday it was still drizzling as we set off on our rounds of the nearby farms. That day seemed full of cats. Farm cats all hung around barns and sheds, complaining about the rain. Then, when we arrived back at the clinic, Major Higgins turned up in the waiting room.

I wondered where he'd come from. I have never been able to find out where Higgins lives. I can track most animals, but Higgins travels along walls and branches, and other places where a terrier can't go. I'm sure he does it on purpose. "We don't usually see you on wet days," I said.

"Very true." Higgins puffed up his

whisker cushions. "No self-respecting cat goes out in the rain without a good reason."

"What's *your* good reason?"

"I heard a python is terrorizing the town," said Higgins. "I need to know the details."

He twitched his tail. "The **clowder** must be informed."

> **Clowder**
> (CLOUD-er) – A group of cats.

I shook myself, spraying raindrops over Higgins. It was an accident, but he twitched his tail at me. "Do that again, Trump, and I'll demote you."

"You can't demote me," I said. "I'm not under your command."

Higgins sniffed. "I remember a time when dogs knew their places," he muttered. "Now, what about this python? Report, Trump. Where, when and why did it escape?"

I told him what I had learned from Whiskey, Hayley, Davie and Dr. Jeanie. "It isn't terrorizing the neighborhood," I explained. "Nobody seems to have seen it since it escaped. It's lost and probably frightened."

"A frightened animal is often dangerous," reminded Higgins. "You know that."

"You're right. But it's my duty to help any animal in trouble," I said.

"It's not your duty to get bitten or swallowed," said Higgins. "My advice is to stay far away from this creature, Trump. Let the humans handle it. Dismissed."

As usual, I was halfway out of the waiting room before I remembered Higgins had no right to dismiss me. I turned to tell him so, but Higgins had disappeared. I knew he was somewhere around, because I could still smell him, but some patients had arrived, so I had work to do.

The first was Primrose the Persian, who came to have her teeth cleaned again. As always, she spat and hissed at Dr. Jeanie.

Primrose wasn't happy about the wet weather, and her furry face looked sour.

I jumped up on my stool. It's in an alcove in the examination room, so I can communicate with the patient on the table without getting in the way. "Don't be foolish, Primrose," I said as she **caterwauled**. "You know Dr. Jeanie won't hurt you."

> **Caterwauled**
> (CAT-er-wall'd)
> – Made a loud wailing noise.

"What would you know, Dog?" spat Primrose. "Nobody does horrible things to your teeth."

I licked my whiskers. "I chew

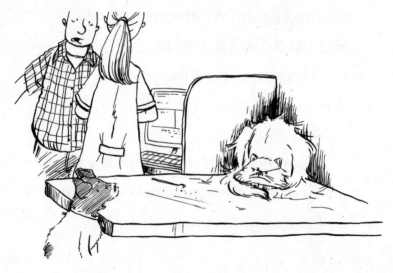

bones and eat good food," I explained. "Also, I am a young dog, so I have young teeth. Calm down. This won't take long if you cooperate."

While Primrose considered that, Al, her person, asked Dr. Jeanie about the python. "Is this escaped snake dangerous to our cats?"

"Cats?" said Dr. Jeanie. "I thought Primrose was your only pet."

"My wife's sister is staying with us, and she brought her Siamese," said Al. "He's a bit of a wanderer."

"I doubt if the python would bother cats," said Dr. Jeanie. "It isn't fully grown."

"It could be dangerous though?"

"It *could* be," said Dr. Jeanie. "But most animals can be dangerous if they feel threatened." She pulled her hand back as Primrose lifted a pawful of claws. "Even cats."

"Stop that," I said sternly to Primrose. To take her mind off using her claws, I warned her about the python.

Primrose flickered her ears. "If it tries to eat *me*, I'll dig my claws into it," she said, as Dr. Jeanie handed her to Al.

Our next patient was my old friend Thomasina. "Hello, Cranky Paws!" I said, as Olivia Barnstormer let the tortoiseshell cat out of her pet carrier and set her on the table.

"Hello to you, Trump." Thomasina waved her tail, then sat down and washed her front paw. When I first knew her, she was hurt

and scared and she hated everyone.
Now she has a good home, so she is
a happier and nicer cat.

"How's Thomasina today?" asked
Dr. Jeanie, smiling at Olivia.

Olivia smiled back. "She's been
scratching her ear." As she spoke,
Thomasina lifted her hind leg and
scratched at her ear, then shook her
head. "It itches," she told me.

"I expect
you have **ear
mites**," I said.

Thomasina's
tail twitched
in disgust.

"Don't worry.
Dr. Jeanie will
look inside

Ear mites—Tiny
insects that live
inside animals'
ears. They cause
itching and
infection. They
mostly affect
younger cats.

your ears and then flush them with warm water. She will probably give Olivia some drops to put in your ears," I explained. "It will feel squelchy, but the itch will soon go away."

"Good." Thomasina tilted her head so Dr. Jeanie could look inside. She even purred a bit.

"You have done wonders with this cat, Olivia," said Dr. Jeanie, when she finished Thomasina's treatment.

Olivia smiled again. "I'm glad I adopted her. By the way, what's all this about a missing python? Is it dangerous?"

Dr. Jeanie laughed. "Everyone wants to know that! I checked some information, and it seems likely Diamond is quite large. He'd eat rats or rabbits, perhaps."

"What about cats?" asked Olivia.

"Yes, what *about* cats?" said Thomasina to me.

"It seems unlikely," said Dr. Jeanie, "but he could still give a nasty bite. Python bites can get infected. If you see him, or even suspect he's nearby, you should contact his owner. The details are on the poster in the waiting room."

Olivia looked worried. "How would I know if he was around?"

"If Thomasina seems nervous, or if you hear birds fussing, then you might check. Don't try to catch him, though. Contact Hayley Seeney and keep an eye on the spot."

"All right."

"Do you know what a python looks like?" I asked Thomasina.

"No."

"It's a black snake with a yellow pattern," I said. "If you see something like a fat piece of rope, stay away."

Olivia put Thomasina in her carrier, then patted me. "You've had a bath, Trump! You're all fluffy."

"No need to sound so surprised," said Dr. Jeanie, and laughed.

That afternoon, everyone asked about the python. Dr. Jeanie explained to the people, and I explained to the patients and warned them to keep away from it. It wasn't easy, since dogs and cats are curious. When one of us sees something strange we usually want a sniff and a closer look.

Over and over, I gave the same advice. "If you see or smell something unusual, stay away. If you can, let your person know about it by running back and forth and making a noise. If you get your person to investigate, put up your **hackles**. But stay clear."

Hackles – Cats have hackles as well as dogs. Cats usually arch their backs and spit when they raise their hackles.

When the last patient left, I went out into the backyard to sniff the air. The rain had stopped, and any scent would be easy to follow. I was off duty now, so I could have a trot outside. I might go to the cottage, or visit my friend Dodger

… I might look for something unusual.

I was still considering possibilities

Distress Call – A call given by dogs or other animals when they need help or advice.

when I heard a **Distress Call**.

Trump's Diagnosis. If your pet keeps scratching its ear or shaking its head, it might have a problem. If the ear smells bad, or has a runny or sticky liquid coming from it, your pet needs to see a vet.

ChaPter 5

Distress Call

Off duty or not, an A.L.O. must respond to a Distress Call. I wondered if I ought to alert Dr. Jeanie, but I decided to check things first. Besides, Dr. Jeanie might tell me I couldn't go out, and I hardly ever disobey Dr. Jeanie. If she didn't see me, she wouldn't give me any commands to disobey.

I knew the call hadn't come from Diamond. Since pythons can't hear or say anything, they wouldn't send

Distress Calls like other animals. I slipped through the door near the hospital cages and trotted down the footpath.

The ground was wet. Water dripped from trees and fences, ran along gutters and gurgled through gratings. In the distance, I heard ducks. They love wet weather, and they quacked duck-songs about the wonderful rain.

"Rain, RAIN, rain!
Splatter on the ground.
Waddle, FLAP, quack
to the splashy, sploshy sound.
Rain, RAIN, rain!
Puddles on the grass.
Waddle FLAP, quack,
while the pond is filling fast."

The Distress Call was not from a duck. It was not from a dog, either. I thought it was probably from a cat. Most cats dislike wet weather. All the cat patients (and Higgins) had complained today.

I put on more speed. The path splashed under my paws. I hoped Dr. Jeanie wouldn't bathe me again when I went home. I passed the spot where the python tank broke, and galloped on. I ran over the bridge, then stopped.

The Distress Call had come from somewhere nearby. Some animal was in trouble, but who? And where?

I cast around, sniffing and listening. Frogs croaked happily in the wet grass. Like ducks, frogs love the rainy weather.

"Concentrate, Trump!" I told myself. "Don't worry about the ducks and frogs. Someone is in trouble."

I shook my head until my ears flapped, then listened again. I knew I was in the right place, but I couldn't see anyone. I barked. "Is someone there? It's Trump, Dr. Jeanie's A.L.O. from Pet Vet. I heard your Distress Call and I've come to help you!"

A cat yowled.

"Owwwwwwongwongwong ..." The sound echoed as if the cat was shut in a bathroom or a cupboard. There were no buildings here, though.

"I hear you," I said. "But where are you?"

"Owwwwwwwongwongwong ..."
came the Distress Call again. It
sounded like it was coming from
somewhere in front of me, and also
below. I ran down the shoulder
of the bridge and sniffed around.
The mud I'd trotted through on
Saturday was underwater now.
Most of the grass was covered, too.
As I watched, some tips of grass
disappeared. The water was rising.
Was the cat trapped somewhere
under the bridge? I looked up, but
the shadows were too deep for me
to see much.

"Where are you?" I asked again.
Sometimes, when an animal is too
scared to respond, all you can do is
talk to it until it is calmer.

The water kept gurgling and I realized some of it was running through a culvert, a pipe that carries water under roads or along ditches. Some culverts are big enough for humans to walk through, but this one was much smaller. I trotted to the nearest end of the culvert and peered in.

It was a bit dark in there. It smelled dank and musty, but my keen terrier nose picked up the scent of wet cat. "There you are!" I said. "Come on out. The water's rising."

"Owwongwongwong!" yowled the cat. The sound made my teeth feel funny.

"Are you hurt?" I asked.

"MowwwwWowoooowwwch!"

By now I was a bit exasperated. The cat didn't sound as if it was ill, or in pain. It sounded frightened and angry. A few spots of rain splashed on my head. I moved forward, putting my front paws inside the culvert. "Come out!" My voice echoed back, making me jump.

"No!" yowled the cat.

At least it answered me this time.

"Why not? Are you stuck? Are you hurt?"

"You're a *dog*!"

"Yes, but I won't hurt you." I tried to sound friendly and helpful. Some cats don't trust dogs. Of course, some cats have good reasons for this! "I'm Trump, the Animal Liaison Officer from Pet Vet," I said, in case the cat hadn't understood when I introduced myself the first time.

"Dogs don't talk to cats. They don't know how."

"I do. A.L.O.s know how to talk to all sorts of animals." The water had been splashing around my paws. Now it was washing over my elbows. "Do come out," I encouraged.

"I can't!" wailed the cat. "I'm trapped."

Trump's Diagnosis. Some animals like being wet. Frogs and ducks love water. Dogs like spaniels and Labradors enjoy swimming. Cats who live in hot climates sometimes swim. Cats in cooler climates prefer not to get wet.

Cat in the Culvert

I sighed. Sometimes cats and dogs get into narrow places and can't turn around to get out. That's how cats get stuck in trees, and dogs get stuck in holes.

I was about to go farther into the culvert to see if this cat was really stuck or just too scared to move when I sensed someone behind me.

No dog likes being caught by the tail, so I backed out quickly. "What do you want, Higgins?" I asked as I snapped around. I fixed him with a terrier stare.

Major Higgins was perched on a hummock. He fanned his whiskers at me, and shook a front paw. His long plume of a tail had drops of water on it. "Stop staring, Trump," he said, shaking the other front paw. "Pffft! This grass is wet." He swiped his tongue along his side, then spat out some loose fur.

"What are you doing here?" I asked.

Higgins looked shifty. "Why shouldn't I be here?"

"Because most cats don't go out in the rain," I said. "Especially fluffy cats like you. Wet fluffy fur doesn't **insulate** very well. Are you heading home?"

> **Insulate**
> (IN-soo-late)
> – Keep cool or warm by acting as a barrier.

Higgins's plume twitched at the tip. "That's none of your business, Trump." He sniffed, and flicked raindrops off his whiskers.

Another yowl came from the culvert. Higgins swiveled his ears.

"Problem?"

I explained about the cat in the culvert.

"Hmm," said Higgins. "If you were *some* dogs, I would suspect you of chasing the cat into the culvert. Since you're an A.L.O. you probably didn't."

"Of course I didn't!" I snapped. "I don't know this cat. I didn't see it go into the culvert. I just want to get it out because the water is rising."

Higgins hopped on top of the culvert and ducked his head to peer inside. "Identify yourself!"

There was silence, then another yowl.

"Stop yowling and report," ordered Higgins.

The cat said in a frightened voice, "Who's that? There was a dog!"

"There still is a dog," said Higgins. "But Trump is a good and helpful dog. I am Higgins, a major in the clowder. No doubt you have heard of me."

"Of course," said the cat. It sounded respectful. "All cats know of Major Higgins."

Higgins glanced at me and preened. "Identify yourself," he said again.

"Wu," said the cat.

"Who?" muttered Higgins.

"I am called Wu, Major Higgins. Peter Wu."

"Then come out of that culvert, Wu. Hiding in culverts is not dignified."

"I can't get out," said the cat. "I'm trapped."

By now the water was chilling my belly. Higgins leaped off the culvert, and up onto the shoulder of the bridge. He dipped his plumy tail to get his balance and looked down at me. "I'll check the other end," he said.

I watched him scramble up the bridge. His tail waved against the skyline, and then he vanished.

I peered into the culvert again. "What's trapped you, Peter Wu?" I asked. "Is it just the water? I know you don't like water, but you can come through it if you're brave."

Peter Wu didn't answer. He just

wailed quietly to himself.

"Higgins has gone to see if there's another way out," I explained. "You have to get out soon. The water's getting deeper." It was getting colder, too. My paws were quite chilly. I am an excellent swimmer, but I didn't want to go swimming today.

Higgins came back. "The other end has heavy metal grating on it," he said. "Not even a cat could get through that. Wu will have to come out this end."

"Tell him, then," I said.

"*You* tell him," said Higgins. "I have to go."

"You can't leave now!" I protested.

"I have to," he said. "The iron horse will leave soon."

"You mean, the train," I said.

"I *mean*, I have to be somewhere," said Higgins. "You can take care of the culvert situation."

"But this cat won't even talk to me!"

"Harrumph!" said Higgins. "You are an Animal Liaison Officer, Trump, so liaise." A large raindrop hit him on the nose and he sneezed. "I have every faith in you, Trump."

"Peter Wu hasn't," I said. I waited to see what Higgins would say to that, but he just swarmed up the shoulder of the bridge and disappeared.

Trump's Diagnosis. Most dogs stay near their homes, but cats like to wander around, especially at night. Some people make their cats stay inside at night. This keeps the cats safe, and also saves small animals and birds from the cats.

CHAPTER 7

Peter Wu

"Peter Wu?" I called. "Did you hear what Higgins said?"

"No," said Peter Wu.

"I think you did," I said. "He said he trusts me to help you. It's getting cold and wet out here and if you stay in there you'll get washed against the mesh on the other end of the culvert. That would hurt."

Peter Wu didn't answer. I thought about going to fetch Dr. Jeanie or Davie, but that would take time.

Besides, what could they do? They were too big to fit in the culvert. They could tempt Peter Wu with treats and kind words, but he didn't seem a trusting cat.

I decided to crawl into the culvert and assess the situation. If sticks or mud had blocked Peter Wu's way back, I could dig him free. Terriers are excellent diggers. If Peter Wu was caught in a net or some other rubbish, I could chew through it. Terriers are excellent chewers. If he was just being silly and stubborn, then I would *chase* him out. Terriers are excellent chasers.

"If you don't come out now, I'll come in," I said. I waited to see what would happen. If Peter Wu came racing out I didn't want to meet him head-on in the culvert.

"Owwongwongwong!" Peter Wu began to yowl again. The noise hurt my sensitive ears. I realized Peter Wu was an **oriental** cat. I knew I must be careful. Oriental cats are intelligent and sometimes fierce.

> **Oriental** (Or-ee-EN-t'l) – Breeds of cats that came originally from China or Thailand, such as Siamese and Burmese.

I splashed into the culvert. There wasn't much room inside, but the roof of the culvert was higher than my head. It smelled damp and sour. I snorted to clear my nose, and heard a warning hiss ahead.

"There's no need to hiss at me, Peter Wu," I said.

"I didn't, you stupid dog," said Peter Wu. "Don't come in. Go back."

I heard a faint brushing sound. Was Wu twitching his tail, like Higgins did when he was angry? I felt nervous. We dogs have sharp teeth but cats have sharp teeth *and* claws.

I moved forward. There were lumps of hard stuff in the culvert that I had to climb over or squeeze around. I think they were pieces of broken concrete. There were also bits of wood that had washed inside. I sniffed again, and caught the scent of a damp cat. It was shadowy in there, but I saw the glint of two big eyes.

As I got closer, I made out the outline of the cat, perched on one of the concrete lumps. He was a narrow cat with big ears and a long, thin tail. The ears were angled back and the tail lashed.

"There you are," I said. I stopped. "You don't look stuck to me, Wu. If you're scared of the water you'll just have to be brave."

Peter Wu spat. "It's not the water keeping me in here, you stupid dog. It's that thing in front of you! It's between me and the exit!"

"In front of me?" I peered at the dark water.

"On that piece of wood!" hissed Peter Wu.

I looked hard at the wood. It

was one of the pieces that had been
washed into the culvert, and it stuck
out of the water. I stretched forward
to prod it with my nose.

"Don't annoy it!" squalled Peter
Wu.

I pulled my nose back just in
time. There was a snake between
the cat and me! Of course, I should

have smelled it before, but there were so many scents in the culvert I hadn't noticed that one. Also, I'd been concentrating on Peter Wu.

The snake hissed, hunching and sliding. Now that I was looking straight at it, I couldn't believe I hadn't noticed it immediately. I bounced back out of range. "It's the escaped python everyone has been looking for," I said to Peter Wu. "Why didn't you warn me it was in here?"

"I told you not to come in," said Peter Wu.

"You didn't even tell Higgins!" I snapped. I wished I was back at Pet Vet.

"No one told me, either," said

Peter Wu. He flickered his ears. He sounded cranky, but I could tell he was cold and afraid. "I want my basket and my cushion," he muttered.

The python heaved again. I knew it was also cold and afraid. What did it want? A nice new tank? That made three of us who wanted to be somewhere else.

"This python is called Diamond," I said. "It isn't wild. It belongs to a nice person called Hayley."

Peter Wu's tail lashed. "It can just go away back to its person then."

"It doesn't know where to go," I said. I told Peter Wu what had happened to Diamond. "Just think if you were thrown out of your basket in a strange town!"

"This *is* a strange town," said Peter Wu. "I'm staying in a strange house with a grumpy cat called Primrose."

"I've heard about you," I said. "You live with Al's wife's sister. But Primrose isn't a problem. This python is a problem."

Peter Wu flattened his ears.

"Maybe I can help," I said. "I think you will be safe if you come slowly past Diamond and don't make sudden moves. Then, when you're out, I can go and get Dr. Jeanie and she can get Hayley."

Peter Wu shivered. "What if it bites me?"

"I'll attract its attention," I said.

"If it's looking at me, it won't look at you." I hoped I was right about that.

I moved forward again. Whiskey had said Diamond couldn't hear, but the python raised his head as I approached. I could tell he was looking at me. His forked tongue flickered, but I had no idea what he was thinking.

Body language – The way people and animals use their bodies to show their emotions.

I can tell a lot from the **body language** of most animals, but this was the first time I had been close to a snake. It was a new experience.

I felt myself quivering with excitement. Diamond stretched

forward. He seemed curious about me. Or maybe he was looking for something warm to snuggle up to.

"Peter Wu," I said quietly, "you should leave *now.*"

I saw Peter Wu put out a paw and pull it back, dripping.

"*Now,*" I said again.

Peter Wu gathered himself together and leaped into the water. It splashed over me and Diamond, and Diamond drew his head back and hissed. Peter Wu jumped again. I heard him squalling as he shot out into the open air. Some cats just don't like water.

Trump's Diagnosis. Different animals have their own ways of expressing things. Friendly cats rub against human legs or other animals. Cross dogs snarl or snap. Pythons are more difficult to understand, but they hiss if they are angry or hungry. Never touch any python unless its person says you may.

DiamonD

The python seemed upset by all the splashing. He hissed again, showing his fangs.

"It's all right, Diamond," I said. "I know you can't hear me, but I'm not here to chase you." I hopped back a bit. "Just stay here quietly and I'll get someone." Still moving slowly, I managed to turn myself around in the culvert, and splashed back to the entrance. The light seemed very bright and I blinked hard. It was still raining, and I shook myself, spraying water around.

A loud hiss made me bounce around. Had Diamond followed me? No. A Siamese cat with blue eyes and dark **points** sat under the bridge.

"Hello, Peter Wu," I said. "I thought you'd gone home."

"I'm going," said Peter Wu. He jumped

Points – On an animal, points are darker patches of fur or hair on faces, legs and tails.

down beside me. "I wanted to be sure you got out of there," he added. Before I could answer, he rubbed his face against mine, flicked his dark tail, and swarmed up to the bridge.

I splashed back up to the footpath

and ran home to Pet Vet. A single strange
car was parked by the clinic, but I ran
past and scratched at the door.

"Trump!" Dr. Jeanie was waiting
for me, and she wasn't pleased. "You
mustn't go off like that!" she scolded.
She bent to pick me up, but I dodged
away and ran back a little way. Dr.
Jeanie called, but I stayed out of reach.

"Oh, all right!" said Dr. Jeanie. "I

suppose you've found some animal or other." She turned to face back into the clinic. "Hayley, Trump's come home. She's found something, and I won't get any peace until I go and see what it is."

Hayley Seeney appeared beside her. "Do you think it's Diamond?"

"Maybe," said Dr. Jeanie. "But don't get your hopes up. It's just as likely to be a cat in a tree or a runaway goat or stray duck. Trump is always nosing around for animals in trouble."

"That's a useful habit for a vet's dog," said Hayley.

Dr. Jeanie smiled. "It is, isn't it? I'll put my coat on and get my bag. Are you coming? We'd better go now before it gets dark."

Hayley nodded. She put on the same long coat she'd worn before, and she and Dr. Jeanie followed me. We crossed the bridge, then I led the way down the slope and peered into the culvert, whining to get Dr. Jeanie's attention. The culvert was nearly full of water now. I was glad Peter Wu had got out when he had. But what about Diamond?

Dr. Jeanie had a powerful flashlight in her bag. She shone it into the culvert. Hayley peered along the beam. "There's a lot of rubbish in there," she said.

I whined and pawed at the culvert, quivering and sniffing. I hoped I wouldn't have to go back inside.

"There's *something* in there," said Dr. Jeanie. "We'd better check the other end."

Hayley looked worried, but nodded. "If Diamond was a dog or a cat, I could call him," she said. "It's difficult to get a python's attention, unless he's hungry and you bring him food."

I followed Dr. Jeanie and Hayley down to the other end of the culvert and saw the grating Higgins had mentioned. Dr. Jeanie shone the torch through the gaps. Almost at once, Hayley cried out, "Look! He's just there!"

I got up on my hind legs to look. The water must have washed Diamond off his perch because he was swimming, bumping at the grating. The water was coming through quite slowly, because of the wood and debris washing against the grate.

"He'll get hurt if he goes on doing that," said Dr. Jeanie. "We'd better pull the grating off if we can. Are you ready to catch him?"

I pricked up my ears. So, Dr. Jeanie could get the grating off? Higgins and I hadn't thought of that!

Hayley pulled on some heavy gloves, and she and Dr. Jeanie unclipped the grating. As it came free, a mass of debris washed out. With it, twisting and squirming, came Diamond.

"Got him!" Hayley was dripping and muddy, but she smiled as she held the python. Diamond whipped around a bit then suddenly slid his

head along Hayley's arm and began
to glide up her sleeve. "He's trying to
get warm," said Hayley, as Diamond's
head popped up near her neck.

Dr. Jeanie stared. "Well ... I'm glad
he's coiling around you and not me!"

"He feels safe with me," said Hayley.
"Do you have a bag or a box I can put
him in while I fetch the new tank?"

We all went back to Pet Vet, and
Dr. Jeanie found an old fish tank.

Hayley put the python in and closed the lid. "I'll be right back with a proper carrier," she promised. "It's the one he should have been in in the first place."

When Hayley had driven away, Dr. Jeanie and I looked at Diamond. Now I could see him clearly. He could see me, too. He slid up close to the glass and stared. I wondered what he was thinking.

Dr. Jeanie walked around the tank. "He looks all right," she said to me. "No injuries. He's a lucky reptile though. He could have been badly hurt if we hadn't found him in time, and I wouldn't want to stitch up a wounded snake." She smiled at me. "Come on, Trump." I waited for praise, but Dr. Jeanie said, "You need a bath. You also need a big treat."

A few days later, Higgins was back at Pet Vet. He waved his tail at me. "Congratulations, Trump. Your mission was successful."

"Yes, we rescued the python from the culvert," I said.

Higgins sniffed. "Not *that* mission, Trump. I mean Wu. He informs me you drew the enemy out while he escaped to spread the news to the clowder. The danger is averted." Higgins gave his whiskers a quick swipe with his paw. "Keep on as you are, Trump, and I might promote you. But for now you are dismissed."

I stayed where I was.

"Dismissed, Trump!" said Higgins. He flipped his tail.

That was too much. I pounced and yapped. Higgins left in a hurry through the window.

Trump's Diagnosis. Pythons are not much like dogs and cats. They are cold-blooded, so they need a heated tank. They eat only once every few weeks. Although they can't hear, pet pythons do become friendly with their people.

About the Authors

Darrel and Sally Odgers live in
Tasmania with their Jack Russell
terriers, Tess, Trump, Pipwen, Jeanie
and Preacher, who compete to take
them for walks. They enjoy walks,
because that's when they plan their
stories. They toss ideas about and
pick the best. They are also the
authors of the popular *Jack Russell:
Dog Detective* series.